Rookie reader®

Purple Is Best

Written by Dana Meachen Rau

Illustrated by Mike Cressy

SCHOLASTIC INC.

New York Toronto London Auckland Sydney
Mexico City New Delhi Hong Kong Buenos Aires

For Charlie
—D.M.R.

To my one and only purple sister, Cookie
—M.C.

Reading Consultants
Linda Cornwell
Coordinator of School Quality and Professional Improvement
(Indiana State Teachers Association)

Katharine A. Kane
Education Consultant
(Retired, San Diego County Office of Education
and San Diego State University)

ISBN 0-516-24187-7

Published by Scholastic Inc., 557 Broadway, New York, NY 10012.

12 11 10 9 8 7 6 5 4 3 2 1   2 3 4 5 6 7/0

Printed in the U.S.A.   61

First Scholastic printing, October 2002

Sue paints with blue.

Fred paints
with red.

Sue thinks blue is cool.

Fred thinks red is better.

"Try blue," says Sue.

"Try red," says Fred.

Oops!

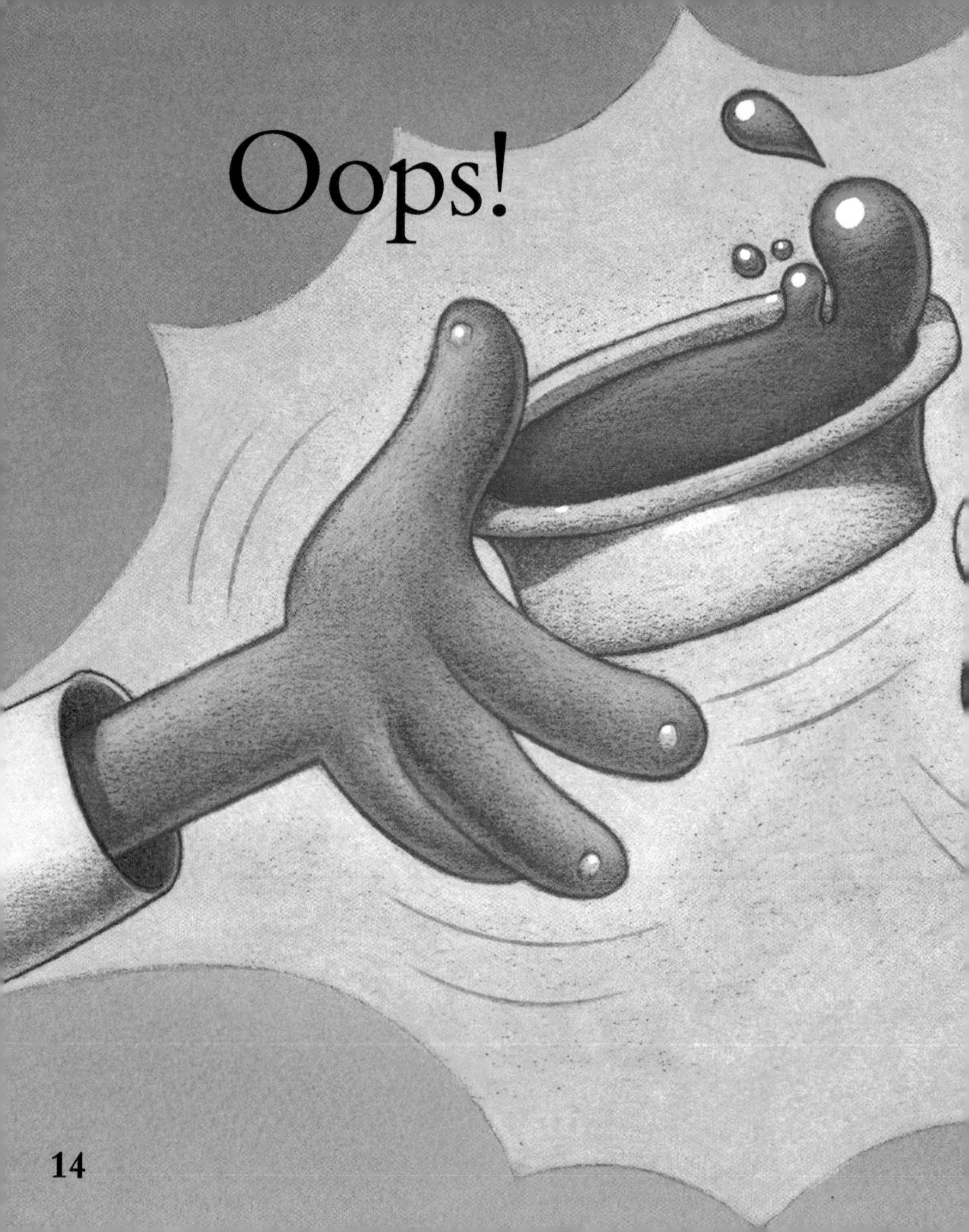

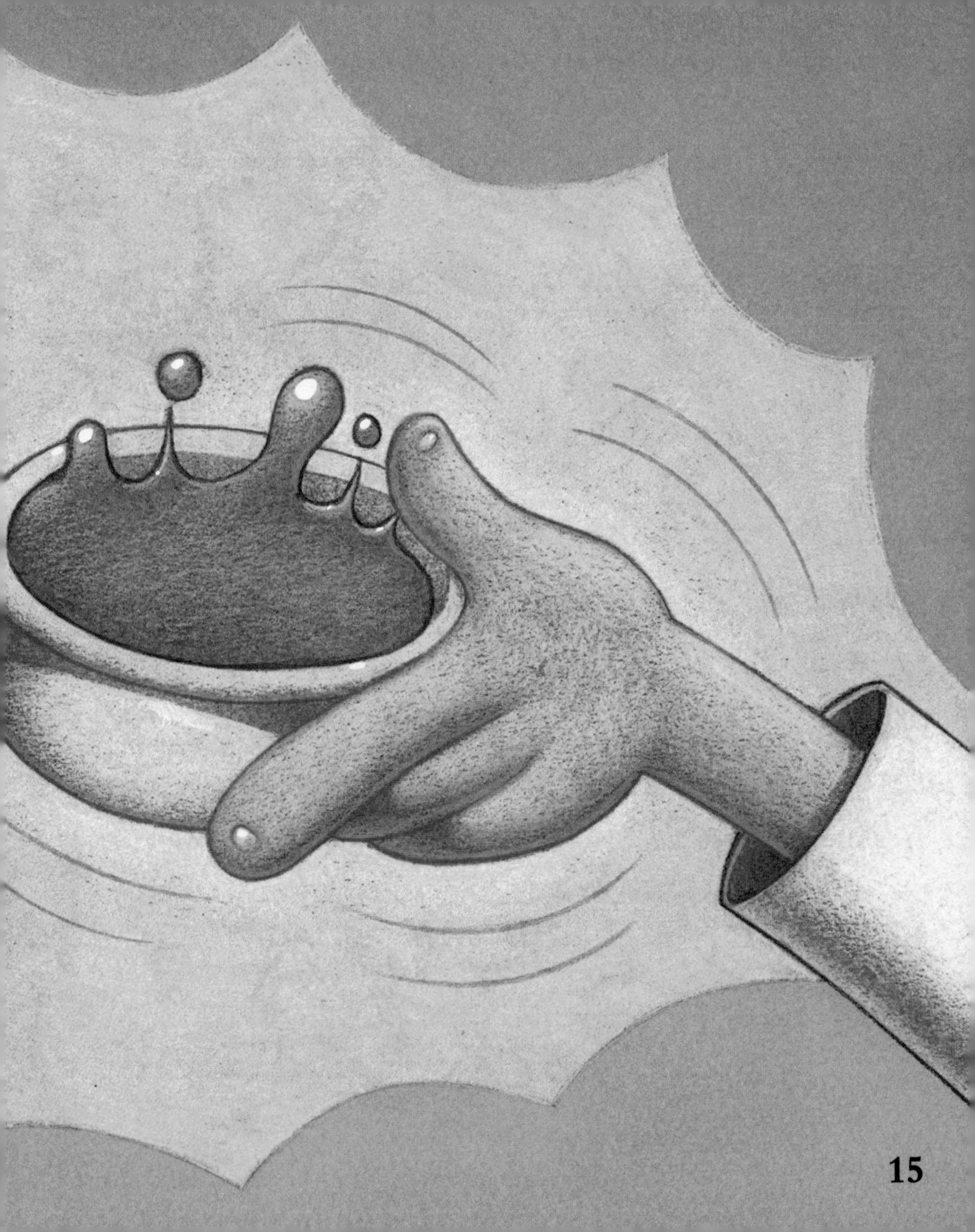

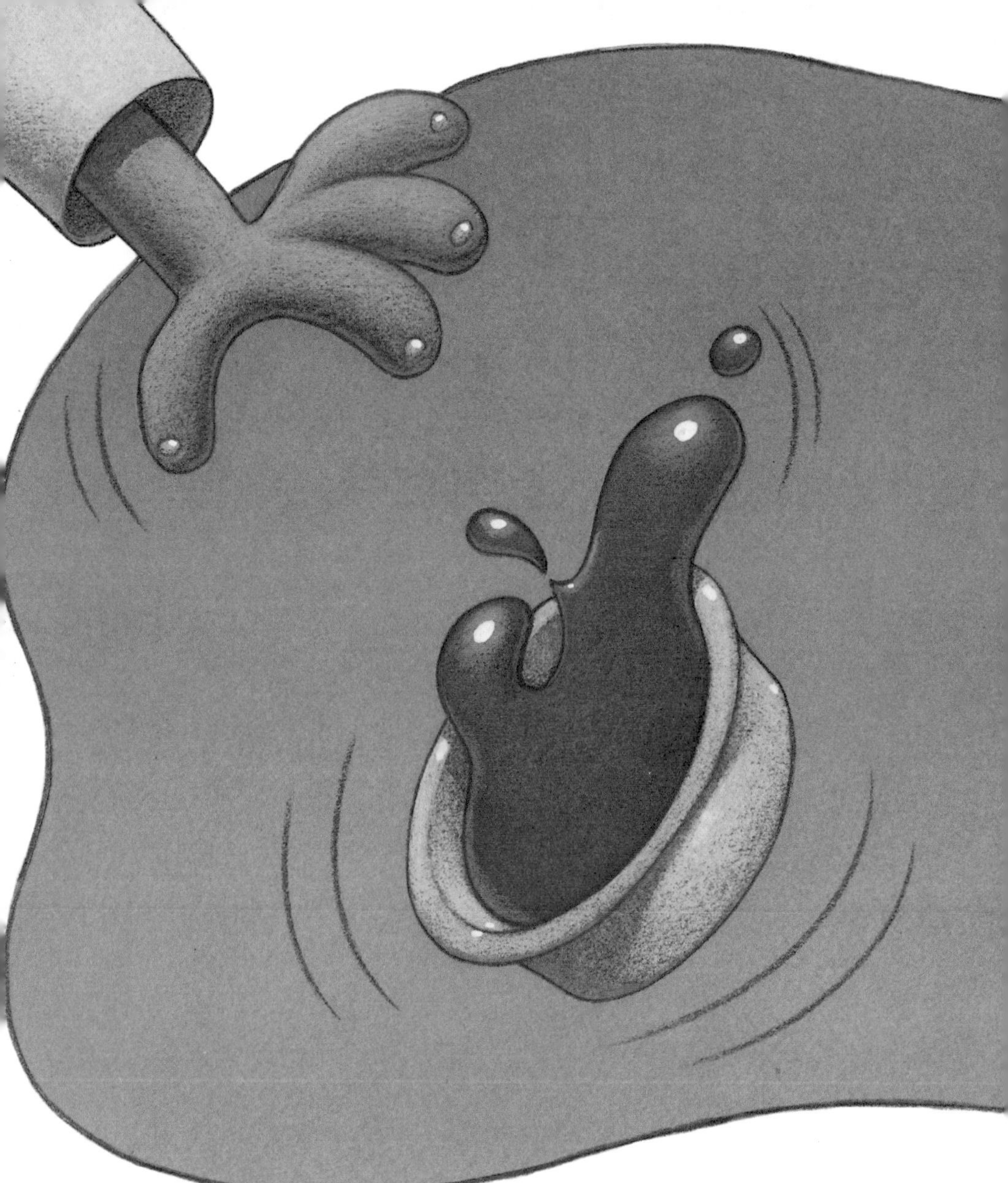

The paint
tips and crashes.

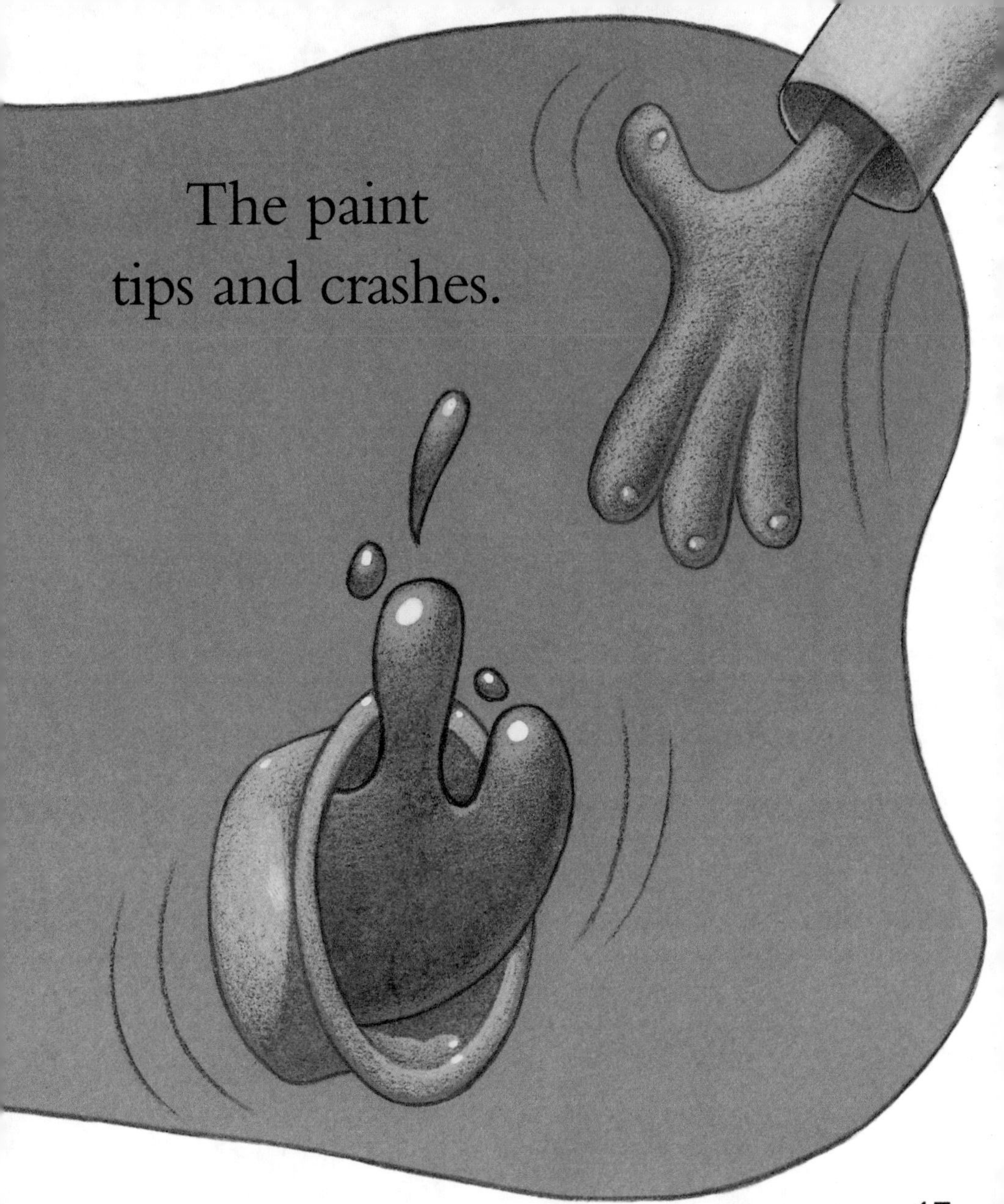

The paint
drips and splashes.

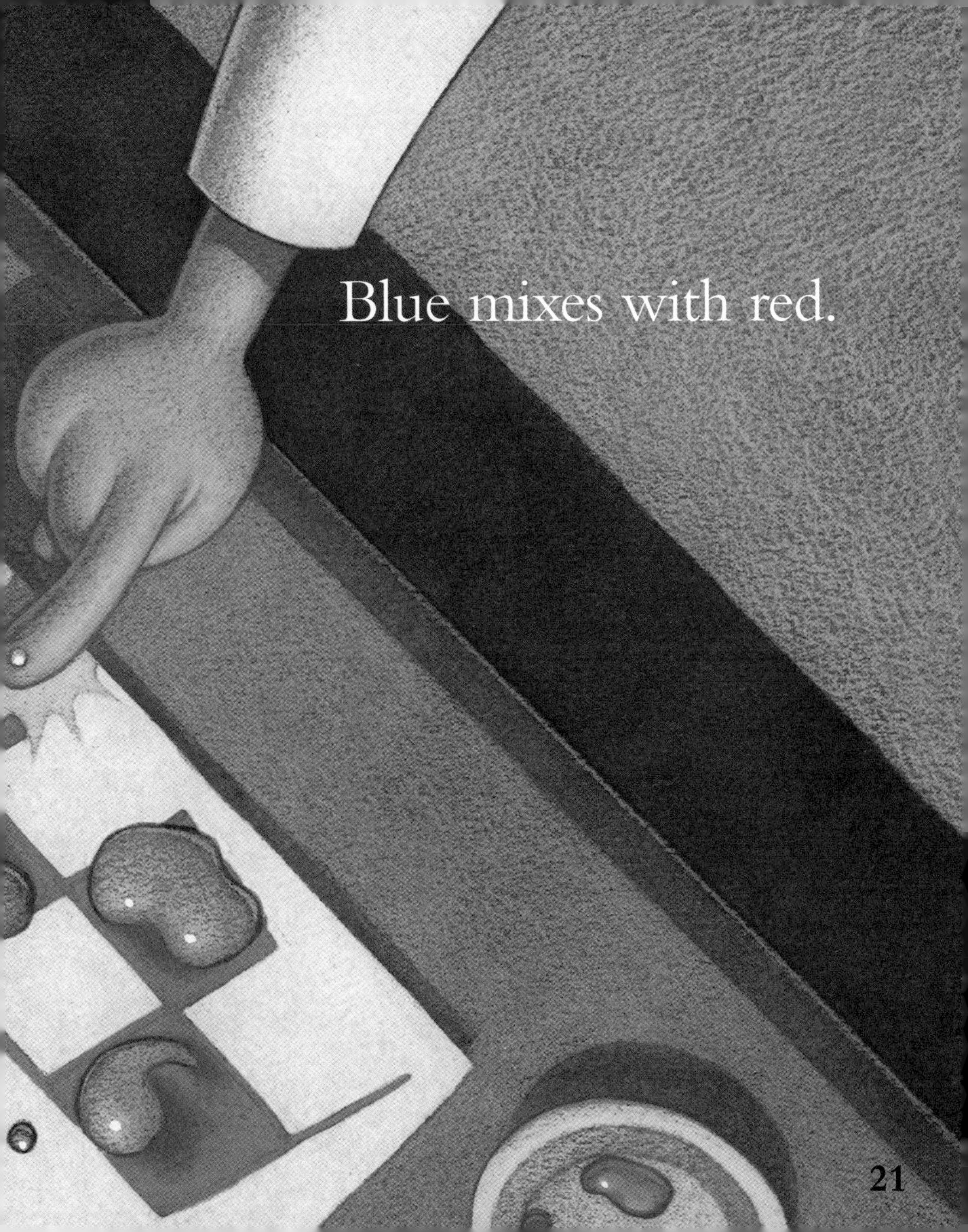

Blue mixes with red.

Red mixes with blue.

Police

The pictures
are purple!

"Blue is cool," says Sue.

"Red is better,"
says Fred.

“But purple...

is best!”

WORD LIST (26 words)

and	Fred	says
are	is	splashes
best	mixes	Sue
better	oops	the
blue	paint	thinks
but	paints	tips
cool	pictures	try
crashes	purple	with
drips	red	

ABOUT THE AUTHOR

Dana Meachen Rau is the author of many books for children, including *A Box Can Be Many Things, The Secret Code,* and *Bob's Vacation* (which she also illustrated) in the Rookie Reader series. She has always studied both writing and art, and loves crafting words and pictures into the perfect story. She also works as a children's book editor and lives with her husband, Chris, and son, Charlie, in Farmington, Connecticut.

ABOUT THE ILLUSTRATOR

Mike Cressy resides in the rainiest part of the United States—Washington State—paints pictures, and tries to stay warm and dry in his hovel, with the help of some hot cocoa.